green kids
Jade Elephant

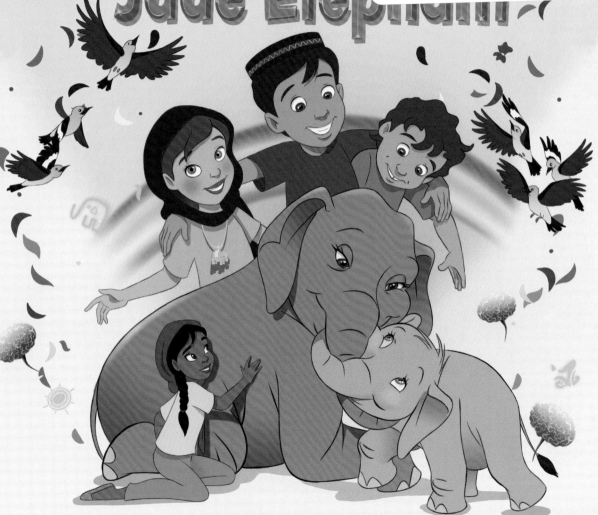

Written by Sylvia M. Medina
Illustrations by Andreas Wessel-Therhorn

1

This book is dedicated to
all the people who protect and care for elephants
especially Save Elephant Foundation.

Save Elephant Foundation

www.saveelephant.org

People were destroying our earth. The Grand Council of Animals met at the magical Green Spring and invited children who love the environment and animals to become Green Kids to help solve the earth's problems. When children worldwide drink water from the magical Green Spring, they gain the power to talk with animals and become Green Kids.

Tiago, Victor, and Maya were the first Green Kids. Now there are many children who are heroes of our planet.

This is the story of Anju, who will help save the elephants.

Maya sat on the steps of a beautiful temple in India twirling about a jade elephant charm on her necklace.

Her brothers Victor and Tiago sat next to her.

They were waiting on their friend, Anju, who was going to take them on tour of her village.

4

"Hey, look!" Maya said, pointing toward the forest.

Her brothers looked up to see Anju emerge from the forest, leading an Asian elephant and her calf!

"Greetings!" Anju said.
"Hello, Anju! Hello, elephants!" the Kids replied.

Maya looked at the mother elephant's face: it was painted with brightly colored designs. "Why is she painted so beautifully?" Maya asked.

"We decorate her to show that she's special to my village," Anju said. "We depend on her to help us work and move things. Her name is Mudahrima, and this is her calf, Gajendra, but we call him Baby Gaj."

Just then, Baby Gaj put his trunk out and began to sniff Tiago.

Tiago took a step back as he laughed. Baby Gaj liked Tiago.

Do you ever ride the elephants?" Maya asked Anju.
Anju shook her head. "Many people ride elephants, but we don't believe that would show them the respect they deserve."
Anju gave Mudahrima a nice rub.

"Are you ready to see my village?" Anju asked.
"Yeah!" Victor said.

"Let's go, then!" Anju replied.
Children and elephants headed toward the forest.

"Wait for me!" Tiago said as he gently took hold of Baby Gaj's trunk and led him along the path.

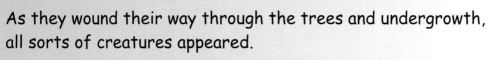

As they wound their way through the trees and undergrowth, all sorts of creatures appeared.

Maya pointed toward a brightly plumed peacock.

"The peacock is the national bird of India," Anju said. "He's so beautiful."

The Kids looked around in wonder.
High above the forest floor, a red panda slept on a
tree branch as turquoise-colored kingfishers and
yellow orioles flitted from tree to tree.

"Look!" Anju whispered as she
nodded toward a thick grove of ferns.
"Do you see the Bengal tiger?"

9

As they moved along, Maya noticed there were fewer and fewer trees. "Anju, what happened to the forest?" she asked.

"We need space to grow more crops," Anju explained. "My father and the other villagers have been cutting down the trees."

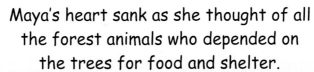

Maya's heart sank as she thought of all
the forest animals who depended on
the trees for food and shelter.

"Anju," she said. "We should talk to your father.
Cutting down all these trees is
bad for the animals!"

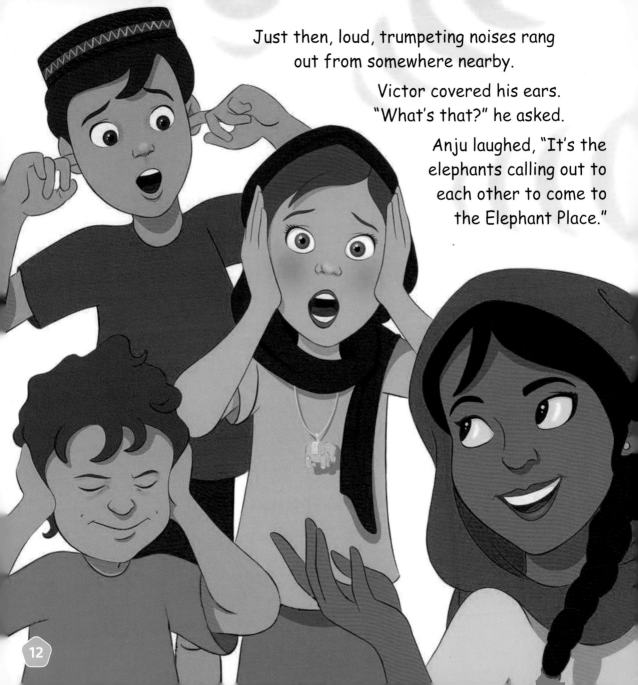

Just then, loud, trumpeting noises rang out from somewhere nearby.

Victor covered his ears. "What's that?" he asked.

Anju laughed, "It's the elephants calling out to each other to come to the Elephant Place."

They headed toward the sounds.
Anju explained, "The Elephant Place is where the elephants and their families gather when there is important news to share or there is a threat to their herd."

Parmita was making an urgent speech to the herd.
"People from the village are cutting down our forest for
farmland and blocking our paths to food and water.

If we don't stop them, soon we will have
no place to live and nothing to eat!
The only food left will be the villagers' crops!"

Suddenly, Baby Gaj
let out a panicked,
baby elephant squeal.

The herd turned and
looked to see where
the noise came from.

Angry at the intruders, Parmita charged toward the children. Anju was so surprised she ran and jumped into the water.

A moment later Anju surfaced, spitting and spluttering.
As she wiped her eyes, she could not believe what she heard.

The elephants were
no longer trumpeting.

They were talking!

"What's happening?"
she asked as she
blinked in bewilderment.

"Elephants can't talk!"

The Kids laughed.
   "This pool is part of the magic Green Spring!
      You can now understand animals when they talk, Anju, just like us!"

Parmita stomped back toward the children.
"Wait!" Maya shouted. "We can help you!"
Parmita paused, listening.

"Give us a chance," Victor pleaded. "We can
convince the farmers not to chop down your trees or block
your paths. There are ways to grow crops without taking more land!"

Parmita was thoughtful for a minute. Finally, she sighed.

"One chance," she said, "but if you fail, we'll eat all your crops!"

The Green Kids and Anju wasted no time. They hiked back to the village to find Anju's father.

"Father!" Anju called out when they saw him. "We must stop cutting down the forests and blocking the elephants' paths to their homes. Please! When you do this, they can't get to their food."

Anju's father looked at her, confused. "What are you talking about, Anju?" he asked.

Just then, loud trumpeting rang out from the forest.

21

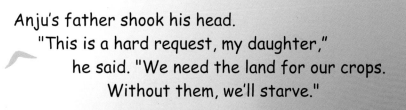

Anju's father shook his head.
"This is a hard request, my daughter,"
he said. "We need the land for our crops.
Without them, we'll starve."

"We can help, sir," Victor said.
"We know people who can teach you about different crops that use
less land, and they know how to set up elephant corridors."

Anju's father looked out at the forest, remembering how much bigger it had been when he was a child. How he had loved running through it. At last, he nodded. He knew the children were right. He would find a way to help the wild elephants.

Anju turned to Mudahrima, "Go tell Parmita that we'll stop destroying her home. We'll learn how to take care of ourselves and the animals at the same time."

At that moment, Anju saw the forest's reflection in Mudahrima's big, sad eyes.

She reached out and stroked the elephant's painted face.

"You want to go home, don't you?" Anju said.

Mudahrima nodded her head.

Anju knew in her heart what she must do.

Anju wiped the tears from Mudahrima's eyes. Then the children washed the paint from Mudahrima's face and removed the colorful blankets from her back.
They did the same for Baby Gaj.

Anju kissed Mudahrima on the head and hugged Baby Gaj one last time.

"I'll miss you," she said.

Mudahrima reached out with her trunk and softly caressed Anju.

Baby Gaj wrapped his trunk around Tiago and gave him a hug.
Then, Mudahrima and her calf left to join the other elephants.

Anju and the Kids heard the elephants making joyful sounds of celebration.

The children quietly crept back to the Elephant Place
and looked in silence at the
majestic elephants.

Parmita spotted the children and nodded. "Thank you for
saving us! Now we can move forward together in peace."

"I'll miss Mudharima, but I know she needs to be with her family," Anju said.

Suddenly, Maya had an idea.

Taking off her elephant charm, she placed it around Anju's neck. "Now you'll always have a way to remember all of us and the elephants," she said.

Tiago, Maya, and Victor said farewell to Anju and headed back down the path toward the temple, looking forward to their next adventure...

Asian Elephants

Photo © Save Elephant Foundation

Asian elephants are smaller than African elephants but still weigh up to 11,000 pounds (4990 kg) and measure up to 10 feet (304.8 mm) high. Females usually don't have visible tusks and not all males have them.

Female and young male elephants live in small family groups while mature males live alone or with other bulls. Elephants live to be about 60 years old in the wild.

Asian elephants' habitat consists of broadleaf tropical forests found in places such as Southeast Asia.

Elephant trunks are like human fingers. They use their trunks to touch, grab, and move things.

Elephants eat grasses, tree bark, roots, leaves and small stems. They also love bananas, rice and sugarcane crops. They eat about 150 pounds (68 kg) of food a day.

Photos © Save Elephant Foundation

Photo © Naturally Wild Photography

How are Asian elephants threatened?
Asian elephants are endangered. As the number of people increases, humans use more land, leaving less habitat for the elephants.

The elephants need tropical forests full of food to survive. But the elephant's land is being converted to farmland, human living space, trash dumps, roads, dams, and mines.

Due to the loss of habitat, elephants have been eating crops, causing human-elephant conflict. As a result, elephants are often killed.

Abuse of Elephants

Asian elephants have been exploited by humans for over 4,000 years. They have been used for harvesting crops, travel, entertaining tourists, and religious ceremonies.

Photos © Almay Stock Photo

Some Asian elephants live as Temple Elephants and are used for ceremonies and festivals. They are often decorated with special paint, ornaments, and other raiment.

These practices are cruel and unnatural.

Photos © Save Elephant Foundation

Save Elephant Foundation

(A Thai non-profit organization)

Save Elephant Foundation cares for and protects Thailand's captive Asian elephant population.

They tackle problems related to Asian elephant abuse in Thailand's logging and tourism industries.

Save Elephant Foundation has established safe parks through-out Asia to support elephants that need a safe haven.

At the time of this writing, Save Elephant Foundation has over 200 elephants under their care. They also take in dogs, cats, and other animals in need.

In addition, they sponsor "Saddle Off", where they convince elephant owners to stop providing elephant trekking and move towards a sanctuary model instead.

Some of Save Elephant's hands-on activities include visiting elephant owners and helping them to learn how to better care for their animals.

They provide food and sometimes take the elephants and other animals to sanctuaries.

Photos © Save Elephant Foundation

Their mobile clinic is deployed to help any animals in need of free veterinary care.

They educate people about the importance of not riding elephants.

Save Elephant Foundation engages local communities to protect the wild elephant's forest land.

They also work with Parliament to establish new animal protection laws.

Lek Chailert: the Founder of Save Elephant Foundation

Lek was born in the small village of Baan Lao, Thailand. Her grandfather was a shaman or village healer. He sometimes allowed Lek to participate in healing animals.

Lek is a small woman with a huge heart! She works with volunteers with government officials to educate the world about elephant abuse in the tourism industry.

Lek is at the forefront of elephant and other animal rights causes, encouraging other countries in the region to save the elephants.

Photos © Save Elephant Foundation

She believes all animals deserve respect and proper care. Because of the COVID-19 pandemic and its effect on tourism, many elephants are not working. They are chained to one spot and may even go without food for many days.

Save Elephant Foundation has worked tirelessly

Lek maintains unique relationships with the animals she rescues. Most days, she can be found at Elephant Nature Park, spending time with the rescued herd.

Many people refer to Lek as the Mother Teresa of Asian Elephants.

Green Kids Club creates books to promote the belief
that animals should be treated with respect and
that their natural habitats should be preserved.

 Storypod

Check out all our Read-Along Audiobooks at:
www.storypod.com/books

This edition designed by
Craftie Fox, Inc.
2980 McFarlane Rd.
Miami, Fl 33133

Contributors -
Kelly Landon
Ryan Emmerson
Charlotte Broussard
Joy Eagle

Medina, Sylvia M.
jade elephant - Storypod Edition / by Sylvia M. Medina; Illustrated by Andreas Wessel-Therhorn,
ISBN: 978-1-953960-17-7 Paperback   -1st ed.
10 9 8 7 6 5 4 3 2 1
Printed in China
Summary: In India, Anju takes the Green Kids exploring with her elephants. The Kids hear a wild elephant
plan to trample Anju's village if the humans continue to take the elephant's land. Includes elephant facts,
photos, and science section.
1. Endangered Species. 2. Indian Elephants.
3. Wildlife Rescue 4. Habitat Management

green kids club

Published by Green Kids Club, Inc., P.O. Box 50030, Idaho Falls, ID 83405